# The Yellow HANDKERCHIEF
## El Pañuelo Amarillo

Written by Newbery Medal and
Pura Belpré Author Award Winner
**DONNA BARBA HIGUERA**

Illustrated by
**CYNTHIA ALONSO**

Abrams Books for Young Readers

New York

My abuela wears an old yellow handkerchief
that her grandmother gave to her.

Abuela scrubs the mud off our patio
on her hands and knees.
Then she sits quietly on the porch and
cleans the dirt from under her nails.

I don't like the yellow handkerchief.

Abuela carries the eggs from the coop into the kitchen.

The smell of homemade
chorizo and eggs
drifts in the air.
My mouth waters.
Becca sniffs.

"What is your grandma cooking for dinner?"

I'm ashamed to tell her. I wish we had money to buy pizza or takeout like Becca's family.

I definitely don't like the yellow handkerchief.

The oldest gallina no longer lays eggs.
Abuela plucks the chicken.

"Um, why does your grandmother
have feathers in her hair?" Becca asks.

I glance at the chicken coop.
My belly will be full, but . . . why can't we
buy chicken at the store like everyone else?

I can't stand
the yellow
handkerchief.

Abuela works in the garden. She gathers tomatillos and peppers.

She moves slowly, but the rows are straight and clear of weeds.

Abuela wipes the dirt
and sweat from her face.

Then she waves her handkerchief to get my attention.
"Mija, ven acá. Ayúdame."

"What did she say?" Becca asks.

I wish Abuela talked like
Becca's grandmother.
"I have to go," I answer.

I despise
the yellow
handkerchief.

"Lava monster! Lava monster!" Becca yells.

¡SEGURO!

I accidentally call out "Safe!" in Spanish instead of English.

I cover my mouth
in embarrassment.
Becca doesn't understand
and springs toward me.

I quickly dodge to one side
too fast, and . . .

Abuela slips off her yellow handkerchief
and wipes my tears.

She kisses my cheek.
"**SER TÚ MISMA,**" she says,
telling me to be myself.

That night, she sits
on the edge of my bed and sings,
*"DUÉRMETE MI NIETA..."*

When my sister, Mariana, gets a bad cold,
Abuela must go live with her sister
so she doesn't get sick, too.
We are all sad.

I move into Abuela's room so Mariana doesn't make me sick, either.

Without Abuela, the room feels so empty . . .
except for the handkerchief.

In all the rush,
she must have left it behind.

The garden is overgrown.
I weed the rows.

Our new chicken squawks. I collect her eggs.

The patio grows dusty.
I make it shine.

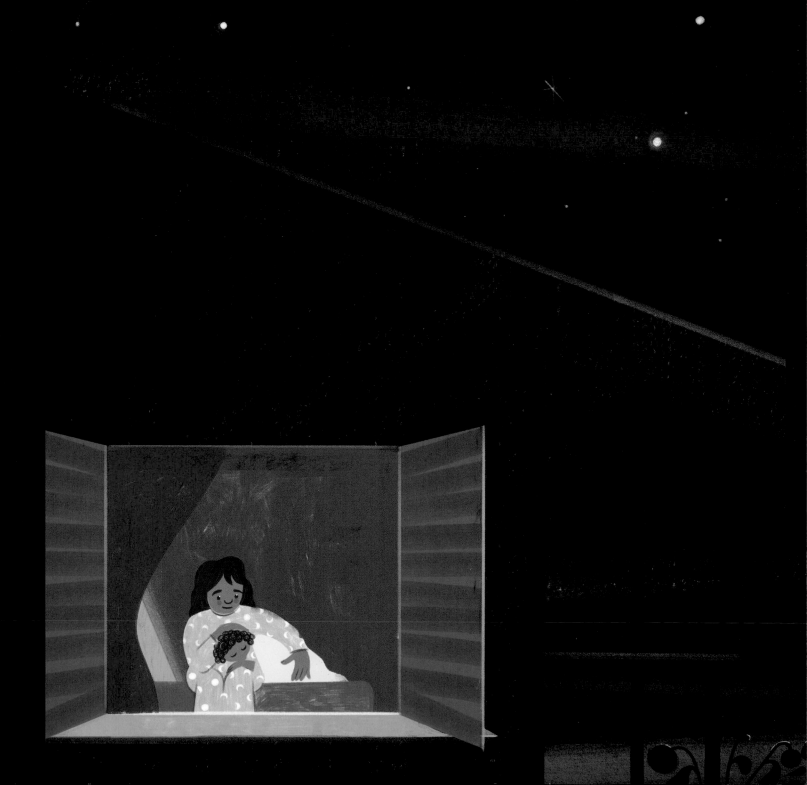

At bedtime, I sing to Mariana,

"DUÉRMETE MI HERMANITA..."

I sit on our porch and
look out at my work.

Without Abuela, I wipe my own tears.

I miss her and I'm tired of us being apart.

And . . .

# ¡YO AMO EL PAÑUELO AMARILLO!

## YO AMO EL PAÑUELO AMARILLO.
## I LOVE THE YELLOW HANDKERCHIEF.

# Author's Note

When I was young, there were things I did not understand or appreciate about my abuela. While my friends' grandmothers wore fancy dresses and drove new cars, my grandmother wore faded housedresses and came to town in an old, rusty truck. When she was a little girl, instead of going to school like other children, she'd worked as a maid in a hotel to help support her family.

My friends' grandmothers lived in big houses with lawns and flower gardens. My grandmother lived in a tiny, tilting farmhouse surrounded by tumbleweeds and cacti in dusty oil fields. Other grandmas had cats or dogs; mine had pigs and chickens (and they weren't pets). Their grandmothers bought their food at stores. At my grandmother's table,

almost everything we ate came from her yard. My friends ate store-bought hot dogs; we scrubbed pig intestines to make chorizo. They had bookshelves of books and traditional fairy tales. My grandmother didn't have a library full of books—but she never ran out of colorful stories about her family and our history. From her memory, she spoke magical folklore that I'd never find in the books in my school's library.

I know now how beautiful, brilliant, interesting, and strong she was.

I miss her stories. I miss milking goats and gathering eggs with her. I miss the smell of corn flour in her kitchen while she cooked. I even miss scrubbing pig intestines to make chorizo with her.

And I'd give almost anything to see her waving her dirty handkerchief and hear her calling me inside just one more time.

*For my grandmother,*
*Maria (Mary) Barba Salgado Higuera Matney*
*—D.B.H.*

*For Hilda and Toti,*
*my beloved abuelas in this life*
*—C.A.*

The artwork for this book was created
digitally with mixed media crayon textures.

Cataloging-in-Publication Data has been applied for
and may be obtained from the Library of Congress.

ISBN 978-1-4197-6014-3

Text © 2023 Donna Barba Higuera
Illustrations © 2023 Cynthia Alonso
Book design by Heather Kelly and Natalie Padberg Bartoo

Printed and bound in China
10 9 8 7 6 5 4 3 2 1

Abrams Books for Young Readers are available at special discounts
when purchased in quantity for premiums and promotions as well as fundraising or
educational use. Special editions can also be created to specification. For details,
contact specialsales@abramsbooks.com or the address below.

**ABRAMS** The Art of Books
195 Broadway, New York, NY 10007
abramsbooks.com